My Best Book of
Animal
Stories

THE BODLEY HEAD
London

A BODLEY HEAD BOOK : 0 370 32546 X

Published in Great Britain in 2002 by The Bodley Head,
an imprint of Random House Children's Books

1 3 5 7 9 10 8 6 4 2

This edition copyright © The Bodley Head Children's Books 2002

Papers used by Random House Children's Books are natural, recyclable products made from wood grown in
sustainable forests. The manufacturing processes conform to the environmental regulations of the country of origin.

RANDOM HOUSE CHILDREN'S BOOKS
61-63 Uxbridge Rd, London W5 5SA
A division of The Random House Group Ltd.

RANDOM HOUSE AUSTRALIA (PTY) LTD
20 Alfred Street, Milsons Point, Sydney,
New South Wales 2061, Australia

RANDOM HOUSE NEW ZEALAND LTD
18 Poland Road, Glenfield, Auckland 10, New Zealand

RANDOM HOUSE (PTY) LTD
Endulini, 5A Jubilee Road, Parktown 2193, South Africa

THE RANDOM HOUSE GROUP Limited Reg. No. 954009

A CIP catalogue record for this book is available from the British Library.

Printed in Hong Kong

Contents

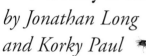

Bottomley the Brave

Peter Harris and Doffy Weir

It doesn't take much to wake me.

So I was on my feet the moment the six burglars broke in.

Of course, they knew they'd made a big mistake as soon as they saw me.

"Quick! run for it!" one burglar screamed.
"That's no ordinary cat! That's
Bottomley!"

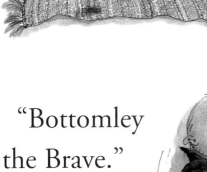

"Bottomley
the Brave."

But I wasn't going to let them get away that easily.

They asked for this, Bottomley, I told myself. And now they're going to get it.

I attacked them in a second, clawing and biting.

Well, the fight didn't last long.

Because I don't think they'd met a cat who knew karate before.

And pretty soon four of them were begging for mercy. The other two tried to run for it.

But they didn't stand a chance.

Who would against a trained fighting cat like me?

And then I just called for the police to come and arrest them.

But the bad news is, while I was clobbering the last two burglars, the other four ate that roast chicken you were saving for supper and escaped.

"You believe me, don't you?"

"No, Bottomley. Not one word.

"But we do believe you are the laziest, sleepiest, greediest, funniest cat…

…who tells the best stories in the world."

The Wonky Donkey

Jonathan Long and Korky Paul

There once was a donkey all tatty and grey. For ten long years he had worked himself to the bone for a cruel owner.

No matter how many heavy pots and stones and logs he carried, not once did the owner thank him.

Never mind thanks – he hardly even fed him.

And at night he gave him a thin rag for a bed.

Then one day, while carrying water home from the well, the donkey's leg went lame.

Immediately he tumbled over, spilling the water.

And when he tried to walk again, his leg had gone wonky.

Oh no!

And he was zig-a-zagging this way and that way across the road.

What was worse, when his owner saw the empty buckets, he went boiling mad.

"You're a donkey that's wonky!" he shouted. "You're not worth a bean. You're the worst working donkey that I've ever seen!"

And he kicked the donkey's bottom once, twice, three times.

So the donkey had to run away lickety split, even though his hoof was hurting.

The donkey zig-a-zag-zigged along the track, wobbling into the verge, and out of it, for miles and miles, until he came to a ramshackle farm where a busy farmer was hurling seeds into the ground.

"Please sir," said the donkey, "have you a job I could do? Just the tiniest job, just for one day or two?"

"Okay," said the farmer, "my potato field needs a big plough. Get hold of a plough and plough that field now."

Well, the donkey did his best.

A thousand times up and a thousand times down he dragged the plough, till his grey fur was completely brown with mud.

But when he had finished the furrows, they weren't straight as they were supposed to be, but twisty and curly.

This sent the farmer hopping mad.

"You're a donkey that's wonky!" he shouted. "You're not worth a bean. You're the worst working donkey that I've ever seen!"

And he kicked the donkey's bottom once, twice, three times.

So again the donkey had to run away lickety split, even though his hoof was really hurting.

The donkey zig-a-zag-zigged along the track, wobbling into the verge, and out of it, for miles and miles.

Until eventually he came to a beach – the first time he had seen one.

And there was a man selling donkey rides for a penny.

"Please sir," said the donkey, "have you a job I could do? Just the tiniest job, just for one day or two?"

"Okay," said the man, "that lady there wants a ride. Get her onto your back and go along the seaside."

Well, the donkey did his best.

He staggered past the beach balls and brollies, but no matter how hard he tried, he couldn't stop wobbling.

In fact, he wobbled right off the beach and into a busy road.

"Help! Help! HELP!" squealed the lady, and the cars started up a terrific tooting and honking.

This sent the donkey-ride man steaming mad.

"You're a donkey that's wonky!" he shouted. "You're not worth a bean. You're the worst working donkey that I've ever seen!"

And he kicked the donkey's bottom once, twice, three times.

So again the donkey had to run away lickety split, even though his hoof was really, really hurting.

The donkey zig-a-zag-zigged along the track, wobbling into the verge, and out of it for miles and miles, until eventually he came to a big house with lots of tall windows and beautiful gardens at the front and back.

A round, red-faced man was standing at the gate.

"Please sir," said the donkey, "have you a job I could do? Just the tiniest job, just for one day or two?"

"Well listen," said the man, "it's funny we met. My girl's lost her cat and she needs a good pet."

And he took the donkey to meet his daughter, Sophie, who jumped with joy when she saw his huge floppy ears and sad eyes.

When he was stronger the donkey didn't mind giving Sophie rides because she was so light.

In fact he did virtually everything for her: digging holes in her sandpit, even pushing her on the swing with his nose.

She always made sure the straw in his shed was clean and his water fresh.

Sophie grew to love him more than anything in the world.

For the first time in his life the donkey was truly happy.

Until one day the father
came running in a panic.
"I don't know what to
do!" he cried.
"Something's not right!
Sophie hasn't come
home and it's now
nearly night."

Without saying a word, the donkey walked out to look for her.
He zig-a-zag-zigged along the track, wobbling into the verge, and
out of it for miles and miles.

Slowly the skies turned grey, then dark, then the rain whipped
down onto the donkey's back like a bad memory.
And then over the howl of the wind he heard...

…a smaller cry.

A cry of panic from the little girl who had fallen into the river.

Without a thought for the danger the donkey plunged into the water and set out for the middle, paddling splish-a-splash-splish with his three good legs.

When he reached his beloved Sophie he shouted, "Sophie my girl, now use all of your might, grab hold of my back and hold on tight!"

And he turned for the shore with the rain in his ears and nose, and started paddling, splish-a-splash-splish.

Going slower and slower. Splish… a… splash… splish. Until with his last drop of strength he struggled up onto the bank.

"Pthew!" Sophie spat out water from her mouth.

But then, just as quickly, tears filled her eyes. The donkey was lying very still at her feet.

She ran back as fast as she could to her village for help.

But when the people came to help, it was too late.

The donkey's long hard life was over.

Gently Sophie's father and his best friend lifted the donkey's body onto their shoulders and carried him back.

It was the first time people had seen men carrying a donkey, rather than the other way round.

And later they built a brass statue of him in the village square: brass ears, brass nose, right down to four brass hooves.

People came from far around to see it. Children skipped, people took days off work, and even the farmer and the donkey-ride owner came to say sorry.

They all stopped and stared, and they nodded when they read the brass plaque beneath. It said…

To remember his limp is to remember just part,
For the wonkiest donkey was the firmest of heart.

Lazy Daisy

Rob Lewis

Daisy was a sea cat.

She lived on a trading ship that carried grain and spices from faraway places across the oceans.

All day she dozed amongst the ropes in the hot sun.

"That cat is lazy!" growled the captain. "All she does is eat and sleep."

Daisy opened one eye, yawned, stretched and went back to sleep.

"There are rat holes in the sails," grumbled the sailmaker.

"There are dirty rat footprints on the charts," moaned the first mate.

"There are rat teeth marks in the salt beef," complained the purser.

"Where's that useless cat?" roared the captain. "I'll throw it overboard!"

"Don't do that, Captain," pleaded the cook's boy, who liked cats.

"Very well," mumbled the captain, "but unless that cat starts catching rats soon, I will sell her at the next port!"

Daisy had been sitting
on the yardarm, listening.
She didn't want to be
a land cat.
She loved the sea life.
She would have to
catch some rats.

Down in the hold, she prowled amongst the sacks trying to look fierce. Perhaps the rats would be frightened away. The rats sat on top of a pile of barrels, laughing.

"Stupid, lazy cat," they said.

One rat nibbled a hole in a sack.

Out poured a stream of flour on to Daisy's head.

"Useless cat!" scowled the purser, when he saw Daisy.

The cook's boy gave Daisy some cheese. "See if you can catch some rats with this," he said.

Daisy climbed into a coil of
rope and waited for a rat to
come and nibble at the cheese.

"Stupid, lazy cat,"
laughed the rats.
They scurried up
the mast and gnawed
through the ropes that
held one of the sails.

Down it came
on top of Daisy.
"Asleep again?"
sighed the
sailmaker, when
he found Daisy.

Daisy crept down to the
very bottom of the ship and
sniffed for rat holes amongst
the brandy casks.

"Stupid, lazy cat," said
the rats. They pulled the
bungs out of some casks.

"Drunken cat!" hissed the first mate, when he found Daisy in a pool of brandy.

"The rats on this ship are worse than ever!" said the captain. "Tomorrow in port I shall sell that cat!"

Poor Daisy. She had never caught a rat before and these were very clever rats.

That night
there was a
terrible storm.
Wind battered
the sails and
waves crashed
over the decks.

The first mate
was at the wheel.
Suddenly he
was washed
across the deck.

The captain came to help the first mate.

"We must steer the ship away from the rocks," said the captain.

Together they struggled to get to the wheel against the wind and waves.

"We shall all be drowned!" wailed the first mate.

Then, through the rain, they saw the wheel.

"Look at that!" said the captain.

"I don't believe it!" said the first mate.

There was Daisy holding the wheel steady with her paws.

She had saved the ship from hitting the rocks.

"Clever cat," said the sailmaker, the next morning.

"Brave cat!" said the purser.

"Well done, Daisy," said the cook's boy.

"I certainly won't sell you," said the captain, and he placed his cap on Daisy's head.

She felt very proud.

And what happened to the rats?

During the storm - like all cowardly rats…

…they left the sinking ship!

Clever Dog, Kip!

Benedict Blathwayt

Hurry up, Fudge, I've got a busy day ahead.

Clever Dog, Kip!

Ellie's Breakfast

Sarah Garland

Come on, Ellie.

It's time for breakfast.

Breakfast for
the rabbits.

Breakfast for
the turkeys.

Breakfast for
the ducks.

Breakfast for
the goats.

The goats don't want their breakfast.
The goats want Ellie's hat!
Look out, Ellie!

But Ellie needs
the hat to carry
the eggs...

to take back home
for Dad to cook...

for Ellie's
breakfast.

The Black and White Cat

Deborah King

 The black and white cat was born in
the city.
 There were no trees or gardens near
her home – only an avenue of streetlights
and paving stones strewn with dirt blown
up by the passing traffic.

Midnight was the safest time for the black and white cat. She prowled the dark streets until morning and then she was gone.

She never saw the sun rise.

In the late afternoon she would wake from her long sleep and look out over her dull, bleak world. She wondered what lay beyond the blue-grey hills.

One night she went further than she ever had before. She walked past the factories and the houses and on and on up the long, winding road.

When she reached the top of the hill the sun rose in a blaze of light.

But it was too bright for the black and white cat who had lived all of her life in the shadows.

Surely I don't belong in such a beautiful world, she thought.

She ran back into the shade. There she caught a glimpse of some strange wild creatures as they scuttled across the forest floor and disappeared.

And from high in the branches, two magpies flew up and up, their wings brilliant against the blue sky.

Cautiously, the black and white cat crept out into the countryside. She hid in the long grass.

Even the insects are more colourful than me, she thought sadly.

Then, in the distance, she saw a herd of big, gentle creatures grazing in the sun. She crept towards them and lost herself in the patchwork pattern that stretched far across the green fields.

She followed them all the way to the farm.

But this was the home of another cat. Wild and fierce, he spat at the black and white cat.

The barn was his territory and no other creature was allowed near.

On and on went the black and white cat, until she found a place where the colours were brighter and more beautiful than ever before.

But could this be a place for an ordinary black and white cat?

She stepped out of the shadows and sat down in the garden. Her coat shone and her eyes sparkled for the first time. They were brighter than any flower.

Someone walked up softly behind the black and white cat and picked her up.

"What a lovely cat," she whispered, taking her inside.

Now every morning the black and white cat looks out over her gentle, green world…

...and in the afternoon she
prowls the countryside in all
her simple beauty.

Who Can Tell?

Stuart Henson and Wayne Anderson

Who can tell
what the trees say
when they whisper
amongst themselves
at the end of the day?

Who can tell
where the sun goes
when the curtains close

and the street lamps
shiver alive
and glow?

Only the midnight
creatures know
what makes the moonlit
garden grow tall shadows
in the frosty light.

And only they keep watch
with the stars
as the colours dim
to black and white.

And one small boy
who every dusk
throws out
a scattering of crusts

and cores
and kitchen scraps
across the lawn
and down the steps.

He knows that somewhere
in the wood,
underground,
in their mound
where the beech roots wind,
the badgers stir.

They come snouting
up from the depths
of the sett,
with their noses first
to test the air.

And the wood is a maze
of criss-cross paths
that go here and there
and then disappear
and begin again.

By night there are eyes,
and the noise
of the scuffle of feet
by the badger den.

In the house, the boy
turns the porch light on
and goes back
to the warmth of the
living room,

where only the fire
flicks and flames
and the garden
becomes a picture
fixed in the window frame.

His mother and sister
have gone to bed,
but the boy curls up
on the couch instead,
and watches the garden
shadows edge
the badgers' path,
their gap in the hedge.

Till at last his eyelids
blink and close,
and despite himself
he begins to doze
as sleep creeps back
and wraps him in
its heavy patchwork quilt
of dream.

Then suddenly
he's wide awake:
Did the darkness move?
Did he see a shape
by the apple tree?

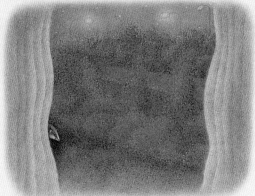

A mistake?

A trick of the light?

But the night
moves again:
it's the stripe
of a badger's face –
and there's two,
maybe more...

And slowly
they snuffle up
to each scrap,
to the porch,
to the big glass door.

The boy creeps too,
to the glass,
where he's nose-to-nose

and he hardly breathes

they're so close
he could touch them,
if only…

and time runs slow

till the last crust's
sniffed and there's
nothing left
and they turn to go.

Down the steps
through the shrubs
to the edge of the light
where they hesitate
for a moment

before they slip out of sight
like children
unwilling
to break a spell.

With a shake
of his sleepy head
he stands up.

Did they know he was there?

Did they care?

Who can tell?

It's Your Turn, Roger!

Susanna Gretz

In all the flats in Roger's house it's nearly supper time.

Roger, it's your turn to set the table.

That's his sister calling.

I see you, Roger!

That's his little brother.

Roger, you know we all take turns at helping.

That's Roger's dad.

...and that's final!

That's Roger's mum.

"OK, OK," moans Roger.

"In other families you don't have
to help," Roger grumbles.

"Are you sure?" asks Uncle Tim. "Why don't you go and see?"

"All right, I *will*," says Roger.   He stomps out of the door…

… and on upstairs.

"Come in, come in," says
the family on the first floor.

"Do I have to set the table?"
asks Roger.

"Certainly not, you're a guest. Come in and have some
fishmeal soup."

What a fancy supper table, thinks Roger…

…but what *horrible* soup!

"Excuse me," says Roger, and he hops upstairs.

"Come in, come in," says the family on the second floor.

"Do I have to set the table?" asks Roger.

"Certainly not, you're a guest. Come in and have some mud pancakes."

What a messy table, thinks Roger...

...and what *dreadful* pancakes!
No one notices as he slips out.

"Come in, come in," says the
family on the third floor.
"Do I have to set the table?"
asks Roger.
"Certainly not, you're
a guest. Come in and
have a little snack."

This family doesn't even
have a table…
Roots and snails – YUK!
Roger hurries away.

"Come in, come in," says the family in the top flat.
"Do I have to set the table?" asks Roger.
"Certainly not, you're a guest. Come
in and have some milky mush."
"Well…" says Roger.
He *is* getting hungry.

Everyone in the top flat is busy getting the supper table ready.
Roger sits by himself
and watches.

If I weren't a "guest",
I could help too, he
thinks.

"What's a guest?"
he asks someone.

"Well… guests
don't really live here."

"Oh," says Roger.
"Now where *I* live…"

Supper time!

Just then a special
smell creeps all the
way upstairs to the top flat.

"Where *I* live," shouts Roger,
"there's something *good* for supper –"

" – and it's my turn to help!"

"I took your turn for you," says Uncle Tim.

"I'll take your turn tomorrow," says
Roger, between mouthfuls.

Worm pie for dessert – whoopee! Roger's favourite.

The Megamogs
and the Dangerous Doughnut

Peter Haswell

In a quaint old shop at the top of a High Street,
a quaint old lady called Miss Marbletop sold
Marbletop's Dainty Doughnuts. She also kept
a mighty, mind-boggling mob of scatty,
tatty, batty-brained mogs. They were called
Miss Marbletop's Megamogs.

One morning, Duncan McDunk opened a rival shop at the bottom of the High Street selling McDunk's Deadly Doughnuts.

Miss Marbletop was mad. "There's only room for one doughnut shop in this town," she muttered. "McDunk will have to go."

But then disaster struck…

Out of the blue, Miss Marbletop was called away to care for her sick sister. "I'm doomed," she wailed as she boarded the train. "The dreaded McDunk will collar my customers. I'll be forced to shut up shop!" Then the whistle blew and the train pulled out of the station taking Miss Marbletop with it.

Kevin Catflap, Captain of the Megamogs, frowned. "That McDunk," he said. "What a skunk! Right then, we've got to beat him and save Miss M. So no lazing, lounging or fat-cat scrounging. No roof-top posing or tin can nosing. We've got serious work to do."

"What's the plan, Kev?" asked Tracy Tinopener.

"We're going to run the shop and keep the customers coming," said Kevin. "So no creeping away and sleeping all day. Come on you cats – let's get back and SERVE!"

The Megamogs went back to the shop. They stood. They waited. They wilted. They sighed. They sagged. But not a single customer came through the door all day.

"It's no good," said Derek Dogbender. "We might as well chuck it in."

"Face it, Kev," added Glitzy Mitzy. "McDunk's done for us."

"Keep your hair on," said Kevin. "McDunk is obviously up to something and I want to know what it is. So tomorrow we're going to find out."

"What are we going to do, Kev?" asked Gary Gristle.

"I'm not saying yet," replied Kevin. "But it's going to be SNEAKY!"

Next day, the Megamogs put on disguises.

Then they sneaked, snukked, sidled and slunk down the High Street

to spy on McDunk, and this is what they saw…

McDunk had strung up a banner
and people were piling into his shop.

Seeing the Megamogs, McDunk rushed out and shook his fist.

"Your daft disguises don't fool me, Megamogs," he shouted. "Hoppit! Scoot! Skidaddle – you barmy bunch of creepy cats!"

"Right," growled Kevin as the Megamogs beat a retreat. "We'll show that punk McDunk! We're going to get Miss Marbletop's customers back. And that means no lazing round with fizzy drinks or sneaking off for forty winks. No yapping, scrapping or catnapping. We're going to do something."

"What can we do, Kev?" asked Fishpaste Fred.

"I'm not saying yet," said Kevin. "But I'll tell you one thing. It's going to be LOUD!"

Next day, the Megamogs got out their musical instruments. Then they climbed into Miss Marbletop's racy red sports car, drove down to McDunk's and delivered a musical message to the people.

"*Buy Marbletop's Dainty Doughnuts,*" sang Glitzy Mitzy and Tracy Tinopener. "*The best doughnuts in the country… doo-doo scoobie-doo!*"

McDunk dashed out of his shop and shook his fist in fury.

"You can cut the commercial, you crummy cats!" he bellowed. "It won't work!"

But it did.

The crowds deserted McDunk's and dashed back up to Miss
Marbletop's shop.

"Aha!" snorted Kevin, smugly. "We did it. We diddled McDunk!"

But he was wrong. Next morning, as
they were preparing to open the shop,
the Megamogs heard a great booming,
blasting and blaring outside.

"There's something going on out
there, Kev," said Fishpaste Fred.
"And I don't like the sound of it!"
The Megamogs went out to look.

McDunk was packing people into a bus to drive them down to his shop.

"*Roll up!*" he was bawling. "*Come down to McDunk's for the best doughnuts in the High Street!*"

Then, when McDunk saw the Megamogs, he bellowed, "You mangy mogs! You moggie mugs! You can't beat McDunk!"

"That does it!" snapped Kevin. "This time he's gone too far."
Then he stepped forward.

"McDunk!" shouted Kevin. "I'm challenging you to a Great
Doughnut Contest. The loser leaves town immediately. Right?"

"Right!" retorted McDunk. "We'll meet tomorrow. Doughnuts
at dawn. And the devil take the hindmost!"

Kevin turned back to the Megamogs. "Now," he growled.
"Tonight there'll be no going out on the town. So…

"…no rocking, raving or misbehaving. No jazzing, snazzing or
razmatazzing. No disco bashing, party crashing, preening, prancing,
sweet romancing, strutting your stuff or dirty dancing. Because
tomorrow we've got things to do. And we're going to start EARLY."

"So pull on your pinnies, pop on your chefs' hats and pick up your rolling pins…

"… no dodging, dozing, ducking or diving. No shirking, lurking, skulking or skiving. Because we're going to make a doughnut that will finally flatten McDunk. And guess what?"

"What?" asked Sardine Sid.

"It's going," said Kevin, grimly, "to be BIG!"

Dawn. The day of The Great Doughnut Contest.

McDunk stepped into the street with a tray of his most deadly doughnuts.

"Catflap!" he yelled. "Come out you flea-bitten bag of fluff!"

Nothing moved. The street was deserted.

Then there was a noise. McDunk looked puzzled.

The noise grew louder. And, suddenly, McDunk saw it.

"Snakes alive!" he gawped. "It's impossible! It's unbelievable! It's BIG!"

This is what McDunk saw…

It was not just a big doughnut.

It was the biggest doughnut in history!

"Captain to ground," said Kevin
Catflap. "Am lowering the doughnut.
Over."

"Ground to Captain," replied Barry
Binliner. "The doughnut has landed.
Over."

"Captain to ground," commanded
Kevin Catflap. "Aim doughnut… and let her roll. Over."

"Ground to Captain," reported Barry Binliner. "The doughnut
is rolling. Over and out."

The biggest doughnut in history rolled down the High Street. Then, as it gathered speed, it became the most dangerous doughnut in history.

McDunk turned and fled. He fled down the High Street. He fled out of town.

A few minutes later...

"Great!" said Kevin Catflap. "Nice Doughnut Contest. But today's the day Miss Marbletop gets back. So nobody takes a rest. There'll be no lounging round and feet-up lazing. No sitting back and telly gazing. Because now we've got work to do."

"Work?" frowned Glitzy Mitzy. "Oh no, Kev – not more work!"

"We're going to make Miss Marbletop a 'Welcome Home' doughnut," said Kevin. "And guess what?"

"Don't tell me," groaned Fishpaste Fred. "It's going to be BIG."

"Worse than that," winced Phil Fleacollar. "It's going to be DANGEROUS."

"No," gloated Kevin Catflap. "It's going to be…

Rabbit Magic

Susie Jenkin-Pearce and Julia Malim

November grey, end of day.
Mist time, smoke time, rabbit time…

...magic time.

Small boy follows
through the gate.

Golden time,
  berry time,
crimson leaves
  in the lake.

Footsteps follow,
  join the chase.
Where to?
  Where next?

Look around.
What's hiding there
in autumn leaves
and evening light?

The moon shines
down as secret
friends dance on
into the night.

Follow rabbit
   through his door,
time is passing
   into sleep.

Falling snow,
   winter time,
peaceful snow,
   feather soft.

Spring sun shines
and small boy wakes,
follow rabbit,
flutter wings.

Buds unfurl and
thrush sings sweet,
the season's green,
the blossom's pink.

Small boy follows
  through the arch,
  to gold and blue.

The spring has passed.

Silent heat
  and poppy red,
a summer's beauty
  will not last.

Danger rabbit! Race through seasons.
Follow small boy back to safety,
back to mist and bonfire burning,
frosty air and warm soft bed.

November grey,
   end of day.
Mist time,
   smoke time,
      rabbit time,

magic time.

Acknowledgements

THE PUBLISHERS GRATEFULLY ACKNOWLEDGE
AUTHORS AND ILLUSTRATORS OF BOOKS PUBLISHED UNDER
THEIR OWN IMPRINTS AS FOLLOWS:

The Megamogs and the Dangerous Doughnut, published by The Bodley Head,
© Peter Haswell 1996

Bottomley the Brave, published by Hutchinson Children's Books,
Text © Peter Harris 1996, Illustrations © Doffy Weir 1996

The Wonky Donkey, published by The Bodley Head,
Text © Jonathan Long 1999, Illustrations © Korky Paul 1999

Lazy Daisy, published by The Bodley Head,
© Rob Lewis 1994

Ellie's Breakfast, published by The Bodley Head,
© Sarah Garland 1997

The Black and White Cat, published by Hutchinson Children's Books,
© Deborah King 1993

Who Can Tell? published by Hutchinson Children's Books,
Text © Stuart Henson 1996, Illustrations © Wayne Anderson 1996

Clever Dog, Kip! originally published as *Kip: A Dog's Day*, published by Julia MacRae,
© Benedict Blathwayt 1996

It's Your Turn, Roger! published by The Bodley Head,
© Susanna Gretz 1995

Rabbit Magic, published by The Bodley Head,
Text © Susie Jenkin-Pearce 1993, Illustrations © Julia Malim 1993